Dear Parents:

Congratulations! Your child is taking the first steps on an exciting journey. The destination? Independent reading!

STEP INTO READING® will help your child get there. The program offers five steps to reading success. Each step includes fun stories and colorful art or photographs. In addition to original fiction and books with favorite characters, there are Step into Reading Non-Fiction Readers, Phonics Readers and Boxed Sets, Sticker Readers, and Comic Readers—a complete literacy program with something to interest every child.

Learning to Read, Step by Step!

Ready to Read   **Preschool–Kindergarten**
• big type and easy words • rhyme and rhythm • picture clues
For children who know the alphabet and are eager to begin reading.

Reading with Help   **Preschool–Grade 1**
• basic vocabulary • short sentences • simple stories
For children who recognize familiar words and sound out new words with help.

Reading on Your Own   **Grades 1–3**
• engaging characters • easy-to-follow plots • popular topics
For children who are ready to read on their own.

Reading Paragraphs   **Grades 2–3**
• challenging vocabulary • short paragraphs • exciting stories
For newly independent readers who read simple sentences with confidence.

Ready for Chapters   **Grades 2–4**
• chapters • longer paragraphs • full-color art
For children who want to take the plunge into chapter books but still like colorful pictures.

STEP INTO READING® is designed to give every child a successful reading experience. The grade levels are only guides; children will progress through the steps at their own speed, developing confidence in their reading. The F&P Text Level on the back cover serves as another tool to help you choose the right book for your child.

Remember, a lifetime love of reading starts with a single step!

Text copyright © 2023 by Amy K. Rosenthal GST Exempt Family Trust
Cover art and interior illustrations copyright © 2023 by Brigette Barrager

Written by Candice Ransom
Illustrations by Susan Hall, Marcela Cespedes-Alicea, and Kaley McCabe

All rights reserved. Published in the United States by Random House Children's Books,
a division of Penguin Random House LLC, New York.

Step into Reading, Random House, and the Random House colophon are registered trademarks
of Penguin Random House LLC.

Visit us on the Web!
StepIntoReading.com
rhcbooks.com

Educators and librarians, for a variety of teaching tools, visit us at RHTeachersLibrarians.com

Library of Congress Cataloging-in-Publication Data is available upon request.
ISBN 978-0-593-56664-0 (trade) — ISBN 978-0-593-56665-7 (lib. bdg.) —
ISBN 978-0-593-56666-4 (ebook)

Printed in the United States of America
10 9 8 7 6 5 4 3 2 1

This book has been officially leveled by using the F&P Text Level Gradient™ Leveling System.

UNI
Joins the Team

Uni the
UNICORN

an Amy Krouse Rosenthal book
pictures based on art by Brigette Barrager

Random House 🏠 New York

Uni is playing
sparkle ball
with Goldie,
Pinkie, and Silky.

Goldie rolls
the ball to Uni.

Uni kicks the ball
high and far.

Pinkie and Silky
chase the ball.

Uni runs around
the silver bases.

"I scored!" Uni shouts.

"Sparkle ball is
boring," says Pinkie.
Uni makes the ball flash.
"I love this game,"
Uni says.

"Some unicorns
are playing soccer,"
Goldie says.
"They need more
players."

"Soccer sounds
like fun,"
says Silky.

10

They all trot over
to the soccer field.

Uni is not sure.
Soccer does not look
like fun.

There are a lot
of unicorns
Uni does not know.

Goldie says they want
to join the game.

"Great," says Coach K.
"You four are on
the blue team."

Uni, Goldie,
Pinkie, and Silky
make their horns
glow blue.

"Keep the red team
from getting the ball
in our net,"
Coach K explains.

A unicorn named Pip
is chosen to protect
the blue team's goal.

The whistle blows.
The game begins!
Pinkie kicks the
black-and-white ball.

The ball lands
next to Uni.
"Kick it to me, Uni!"
Silky yells.

19

But Uni kicks
the ball to a
red team player.
Oh, no!

The red team player
kicks the ball.
It sails toward the
blue team's net.

Uni runs fast
to get the ball
but trips.

Pip looks up.
"I cannot see,"
he says.
"The sun is in
my eyes!"

The ball rolls into
the blue team's goal.

The red team scores.

They jump up and down.

Pip starts to cry.

"I messed up," says Pip.

"I feel like quitting."

"I messed up, too,"
Uni says.
"But we cannot quit.
We are a team!"

Next, a red team player
kicks the ball at
the blue team's net.

Uni wishes hard.

The ball sparkles!

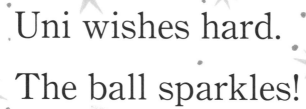

Pip can see it!

He kicks the ball

to Uni.

Uni kicks it
high and far to Goldie.

Goldie kicks the ball
into the red team's net!

"We scored!" Uni shouts.

The blue team high-fives!

"Soccer is fun when
we work together,"
says Uni.
"Go, team!"